Before Night Falls

by

Keith Gray

Published in 2003 in Great Britain by
Barrington Stoke Ltd
10 Belford Terrace, Edinburgh EH4 3DQ

ISBN 1-842991-24-8

Printed by Polestar Wheatons Limited

A Note from the Author

For as long as I can remember I've enjoyed scaring myself. Most of us do, I think. I've always been a huge fan of horror stories. My favourite kind are the ones that freak you out, instead of gross you out. So this book is my attempt to write something spooky rather than gory.

It's also a story about friendship and loyalty, two themes I've written a lot about in the past. Andy, Glen and Megan have their friendship pushed to the very limit, and their loyalty to one another tested in the most extraordinary circumstances.

It's a story that hopefully packs a bit of a punch. It should also be the kind of story that makes you ask yourself, "What would I do if I was there?" Personally, I love that kind of question. But don't blame me if the answer's not an easy one.

And just in case you wondered, the place names in the book are all real. I found them on a map, so you should be able to as well.

Contents

Chapter 1
The Night Before

The cold wind bullied the two small tents pitched on the dark hillside. They stood apart from each other. They had been hastily pegged out, and the ropes threatened to pull loose every time the harsh wind blew.

One tent was silent, looking like just another shadow in among the rocks and tall bushes. There were whispered voices from the other and a jittering point of light could be seen through the canvas side of the tent.

Inside Andy and Glen struggled with the large map. The tent was too cramped to be able to open the map up fully but they spread it out as best they could on top of their sleeping bags. They hunched over it. The map was still damp from the rain and had been ripped along one of its folds. Glen aimed their only torch at where he thought they were.

"I reckon we should be here," he said.

"Yeah, *should* be," Andy agreed.

Glen shrugged. He leaned closer over the map, studying it. "Maybe we came this way." He ran his finger along one of the marked footpaths.

"We would have come right by that old disused quarry if we had," Andy said, pointing out where it was written on the map. "It would have been pretty difficult to miss a massive hole in the ground. Even for us."

"What about this way, then?" said Glen.

Andy peered at where his friend was focusing the torch's beam. "Over that hill, you mean?"

Glen nodded. "We *did* walk up a hill."

"It felt like we walked up *hundreds* of hills," Andy said. Which was true. They'd walked and walked and walked. Just not in the right direction. They'd probably spent all day walking in circles. This was the North Yorkshire Moors, but right now it so easily could have been the middle of nowhere.

Andy had a bottle of vodka that he'd pinched from home, and he'd wanted to open it tonight, but nothing was going to plan. He fiddled with the cap, but didn't break the seal.

"It'll be better in the morning," Glen said, as lightly as he could. He grinned and shrugged his shoulders again. "We'll climb a tree or something, look for landmarks."

Andy gave a weak laugh. "Yeah. It's not as though we're *really* lost, is it? We're still somewhere in Yorkshire, right?"

Glen agreed quickly. "We're still somewhere in England."

"In Britain," added Andy.

"Not *really* lost," said Glen.

"Not *lost* lost," said Andy.

They were laughing, but a sudden gust of wind made their little tent shudder and their smiles froze instantly as they both held their breath. The canvas rippled fiercely, the poles swayed. The wind buffeted the tent and pushed against its sides. They waited for the worst, but luckily the ropes held. Nothing collapsed.

The two friends rolled their eyes at each other in the dim light, and laughed again. Only somewhat more quietly this time.

Andy was grateful Glen was such a good friend, a solid friend. Both of them knew that this situation was probably Andy's fault, yet Glen would be the last to admit it. He was taller than Andy, a bit heavier too, but they both had dark, straggly hair and had been confused as brothers on more than one occasion. They'd known each other almost as long as either of them could remember.

They made a good team. Andy came up with the ideas, and Glen sussed out how to work on them. This was exactly what had happened this time around too. It had been Andy who'd suggested the camping trip, but Glen who had talked the school into letting them borrow the old-fashioned tents usually kept for those doing their Duke of Edinburgh Award.

It had been left to Andy to talk their parents into letting them go off alone, however. He'd told them that he and Glen were 16 and not stupid, 16 and capable of looking after themselves, 16 and smart enough to walk from A to B even if there were a few hills in-between. Although Andy reckoned that there might be a big question about that now.

The wind seemed calmer. "Do you think we should check on Lucy and Megan's tent?" Glen asked.

Andy shook his head. "Trust me, if it had collapsed, they'd be able to hear the screams back home in York," he said.

Glen grinned at this. Then said, "I don't think Lucy's very happy with you at the minute, is she?"

Andy was still fiddling with the unopened bottle of vodka. "No," he admitted, with a small smile. "I don't think she is." The drink had been for her.

This had been what Andy's great idea was all about, of course. This was his brilliant scheme. He'd been seeing Lucy for almost a year now. They both complained that they never really got a chance to be truly alone together. Because there were usually parents around. Because her father hovered over them like a bird of prey. So why not invite her on a camping trip during the Easter holidays, into the middle of the countryside, where even Daddy's eagle eyes couldn't see? And hopefully get to share a sleeping bag with her ...

Lucy had been unsure at first. It was still only April, so wouldn't it be too cold? "Not if we keep each other warm," Andy had told her with a wink, making her giggle.

She'd come round to the idea slowly, and then would only say yes if she could bring her friend, Megan. Which had been fine by Andy. He couldn't have agreed quicker, because he'd thought he could get Glen and Lucy's friend together. Andy had always had lots of girlfriends, but Glen still hadn't had one yet. So perhaps this could be his lucky weekend.

If nothing else, Andy thought, *we should all have a good laugh.*

However, things had not turned out the way Andy had hoped.

The rain had lashed down. Buckets and buckets.

Glen, being as shy as usual, hadn't said more than two words to Megan. Until they'd started arguing over the map reading, that is. Then the bickering had got so heated they'd almost torn the map in half.

When it had started to get dark, Lucy had wanted to call her dad on her mobile. Andy had been thankful that she couldn't get a signal up here on the Moors. Her father didn't like him and would have said at once that everything was Andy's fault. Even the rain, probably. So he'd done his best to assure her they were OK. But she'd got angry and snapped at him. Then it had all become one big shouting match.

They'd pitched the tents as fast as they could. Andy always liked to make the best of a tricky situation and had offered to dry Lucy and keep her warm in a tent by themselves. The look on her face, however, had been enough to stop him from asking more than once.

So Lucy and Megan had crawled wet, worn-out and fed up into one tent, while Andy and Glen had skulked into the other. And this is exactly where they'd been for the past couple of hours or more. It had only stopped raining ten minutes ago.

Andy looked at his watch now. Almost 10.30. He gave a heavy sigh.

"Maybe we should call it a night," he told Glen. "As you say, it'll be better in the morning." He shoved the bottle of vodka back into his rucksack. "I'll save this for tomorrow."

Glen nodded his agreement. They had to shuffle themselves around in the cramped space to be able to fold up the map again.

They were just about to slip into their sleeping bags when they heard the zip on the girls' tent being pulled down and someone suck in a quick breath as they stepped outside into the cold air.

"Lucy?" Andy called quietly. He didn't wait for an answer, but unzipped their tent and stuck his head out through the flap. The wind was sharp against his cheeks. "Hey! Lucy!"

He could tell it was her just by her silhouette against the dark sky. Her long, blonde hair whipped around her head.

"Are you OK?" Andy called out to her.

"Shh," she hissed. "Megan's asleep!"

He lowered his voice. "But you're OK, yeah?" And then, when she didn't answer, "Are you talking to me yet?"

"Yes, I'm OK," she said. "Now that I'm dry again, anyway. But, no, I'm not talking to you."

Andy couldn't see her face, but he thought he heard a little humour in her voice, even above the wind. "Will you ever talk to me again?" he asked.

"I doubt it. It would be against my principles."

He smiled. He was sure now that there was a touch of fun there, however small. It was a relief after the way she'd acted that afternoon. She'd been close to tears when she'd been soaked to the skin and had realised they were lost. But this sounded a bit more like the Lucy he knew.

"It's not your fault it rained." She turned to look at him. Her face was like a small, pale moon in the dark. "I'm cold and fed up and have to go pee. You told me this weekend was going to be romantic. But, funnily enough, peeing behind a bush in the dark is *not* my idea of romance."

"It'll be better tomorrow," he said. "Honest."

She was holding her mobile phone. "I tried to call my dad again, but I still can't get a signal."

That was the last thing Andy wanted. He climbed out of the tent, desperate to convince her that all was well. "Honest, Lucy. It'll be fine in the morning," he said. He walked over to her, and was pleased when she let him put his arm around her. He tried to warm her a little against the chill wind. "At least we can't get lost twice. That would be impossible."

"Hmm," she said with a smile. "Maybe not for you and Glen."

He laughed at her joke to let her know things were still all right. "In the morning we'll—"

But she cut him short. "I need to *pee*," she reminded him.

"Oh, OK, yeah." He hugged her quickly, then scrambled back inside the tent. He was rough enough with the zip for her to be able to hear it and know she had what privacy a night-time hillside could give her.

Glen was already buried in his sleeping bag. "She still likes you, then?"

"Why shouldn't she?" Andy beamed. He was feeling brighter again, and thinking that maybe everything really would be OK in the morning. "So all we have to do is convince Megan just how fantastic *you* are."

Glen snorted through his nose. "Don't bother. She's a right moody cow."

Andy waved the bottle of vodka under his nose. "A bit of this warming you up tomorrow night and you might think differently."

He switched off the torch and slid deep down into his sleeping bag. It wasn't just the vodka he'd brought with him in his rucksack. Tucked away inside one of the pockets was a gold heart on a chain. The back of the heart had "I love you" on it. He'd not admitted this to Lucy yet. The original idea had been to give her the heart tonight, and the vodka was just to celebrate. He fell asleep happy with the thought that there was still tomorrow.

Chapter 2
First Light

Andy wasn't sure whether or not he was still dreaming when he heard Megan shout, "Andy! Lucy's gone!"

He was curled up at the very bottom of his sleeping bag because that was the only way he could keep warm. He'd been dreaming about being on holiday in Whitby with his mum when he was younger, and it took a second or two to remember exactly where he was.

When Megan started shouting, he thought at first it was all part of his dream. But then she was shaking the tent. She sounded frantic.

He crawled out from the sleeping bag and saw Glen looking a bit dopey and still sleepy-eyed as he poked his head out of his.

"What's going on?" Glen asked.

"Andy!" Megan was shouting. "Andy!" She was slapping her hands against the tent's side. "Get up! Lucy's gone!"

Andy scrambled outside and into the sudden chill of the early morning. He blinked against the crisp sunlight, feeling the cold dew on the grass under his bare feet. Megan's red hair was all over the place and her eyes were wide and frightened.

"What—?" he began.

"I don't know where Lucy is," she said. "She's not in the tent."

Andy wrapped his arms around himself. It was freezing, he could see his breath. It seemed to be taking his head a bit of time to get into gear this morning. "She's probably having a pee or something," he said, looking around for a likely bush his girlfriend could be behind.

But Megan was shaking her head. "Her sleeping bag's still rolled up in her rucksack."

"Lucy!" Andy shouted. "Lucy!"

Glen popped his head out of the tent. "What's up?" he asked.

"Lucy's wandered off," Andy told him. He hopped from foot to foot, shivering. He wanted to be back in his sleeping bag. To be honest he was a bit embarrassed by all the fuss Megan was making. "Lucy!" he shouted.

Megan, however, was close to tears.

"I don't think she's been in the tent all night," she said. "Her mobile's not there or anything."

Andy nodded. "Yeah, she had it with her when she nipped to the loo last night," he tried to explain, and yet still didn't understand what had happened himself.

"Didn't she come back, then?" Glen asked.

Andy shrugged. "I don't know. I just zonked out. I didn't hear a thing ..."

And that was when it hit him. He turned quickly on Megan. "Did she come back? Do you know if she—"

Megan shook her head miserably. "I was asleep too. I woke up this morning and saw her rucksack was still packed away and everything and didn't know where she was."

She dug in her pocket for her cigarettes, and her hands were shaking as she struggled to light one.

Suddenly Andy forgot the cold. His stomach seemed to drop away and he swore loudly. "Lucy!" he bellowed. "Lucy!"

He spun in a circle, looking everywhere at once. He thought he must be able to see her. She must be somewhere. Must be.

The hillside fell away slowly with rough grass and clumps of fern or bracken. There were a few scrubby bushes, one or two half-bare trees. But nowhere to hide, nowhere to go unseen.

"LUCY!"

He pulled on his trainers over his bare feet, grabbed his coat and ran up the hill. Glen and Megan were close behind. They were all shouting her name. They leapt over the small boulders in their way, pushing through the tangled bushes. The fear inside Andy was like an icy liquid, running through every vein in his body.

"LUCY!"

At the top of the hill he turned around and around again. The empty North Yorkshire Moors lay before him in every direction. The green and brown hills rolled away on every side beneath the weak sun.

He could see far-off clusters of trees. Hedges chopped up the fields away in the distance. A string of electricity pylons marched across the valley and vanished out of sight. But no Lucy.

Glen was out of breath, panting. "Where could she have gone? Where would she have walked to?" There was no sign of a village, or farmhouse. "Why didn't she tell us she was going?"

These were all questions Andy wanted to ask too, but the ice in his blood was making it difficult for him to think straight.

"She couldn't have gone far," he managed to say. He was scanning the rocks and bushes on the hillside.

Maybe she'd tripped over a rock and fallen down. Maybe she'd knocked herself out. She might be lying freezing in the thick bracken where they couldn't see her.

"Her mobile," said Andy suddenly, turning on Megan. "Call her mobile. We might hear it ringing."

They raced back to the tents and Megan hunted through her rucksack for her phone. She nearly dropped it in her haste, frustrating Andy, who snatched it from her.

He stabbed at the numbers to dial Lucy's phone. But nothing happened. He swore and hit the buttons again.

"There's no signal up here," Megan said. She had tears on her cheeks and was wiping her nose on her sleeve. She was lighting her second cigarette.

Andy ground his teeth. "Lucy! LUCY!" He charged higher up the hill again. It was almost as though the empty Moors were mocking him.

He was more frightened than he'd ever been in his life before, and was blaming himself for everything. It had been his idea to come camping. He'd let Lucy wander off in the dark by herself. He'd fallen asleep when she'd been out there.

Glen was still at the top of the hill. "There! Over there!" he shouted, pointing away from their tents. He was running towards a tumble of rocks where the gorse and bracken was thin. "There!"

Andy couldn't see anything from where he was standing lower down the hill, but he followed the way Glen pointed.

"Look!" Glen shouted, trying to point Andy in the right direction. "There. *There*!"

Then Andy was running that way too, because he could see it now. A scrap of material, brighter than the grasses. And it was a coat, a waterproof. It was Lucy's, he was sure of it.

He found it hard to stay on his feet as he ran across the hillside, scrambling over the rocks and rough ground. But it was Lucy. It was her! There was a huge rush of relief making him feel light-headed.

Glen got there first but Andy pushed him aside.

She was as pale as a ghost. Her body was twisted, her arms flung out. Her hair looked like a splash of yellow across the rocks and her eyes were closed.

"Has she fallen?" Andy asked crouching down next to her.

"Don't touch her," Glen warned. "If she's fallen and broken her back or something we can't move her."

But running through Andy's mind was, *Is she dead? Is she dead? Is she dead?*

He hovered over her, knowing that Glen was right about not touching her, but desperate to shake her, to wake her up.

Megan was with them now. "I know first aid," she said. "Lucy, can you hear me? Can you hear me, Lucy?"

She threw her half-smoked cigarette aside and listened at Lucy's mouth for breathing. Then she placed her fingers on her throat.

"I think there's a pulse," she said. "Yeah. I think I can feel it. But only just. We've got to get her warm, or she'll freeze to death."

"We can't move her," Glen repeated.

"We have to," Megan told him. "Get her in a sleeping bag to warm her up."

"Has she fallen?" Andy asked.

Now that the giddy relief of finding her was beginning to fade, he could see the scratches on her face and neck. They were very red on her pale, pale skin.

"Look at those scratches." He knew what they looked like to him, but he felt stupid admitting it.

It was Glen who said, "They look like claw marks."

They were slashed across her face, a bright and angry red. There were two distinctive wounds on her neck. They were deep, about a centimetre long, and parallel to each other.

"It looks like she's been attacked by something," Glen said.

Chapter 3
Morning Mist

Andy wasn't sure what to feel. The scare of Lucy being missing had been heart-stopping. It had been like a massive electric shock. But finding her in this state left no room for true relief. The panic he felt now was long and drawn-out and somehow even more painful.

The weak morning sun was covered by grey cloud. A thin drizzle hung in the air. Megan had calmed down a lot and brought herself under control, even though there were still tears in her eyes. She did her best to check Lucy for broken bones. When she found none, the boys wrapped up Lucy's icy-cold body in two of their sleeping bags and carried her carefully back to the tents. They tried Megan's phone again and again. But the bad weather and the surrounding hills were killing the signal.

At first they didn't talk at all. They just stood around Lucy's limp body, looking down at her lying in the sleeping bags on the grass.

Then suddenly it was as though they couldn't stop talking.

"Did you hear anything last night?" Andy asked Megan.

She was lighting yet another cigarette. "I was asleep. I didn't even hear her talking to you. What time did you say that was?"

"About half-ten. But I went straight to sleep too." It hurt to admit it. "I can't believe I just left her alone ..."

"Do you really think something attacked her?" Glen asked.

"She *must* have fallen," Andy said.

"But what about those marks on her neck?" Glen wanted to know.

Andy was shaking his head. "No, no." He didn't want to admit she'd been attacked, because that would make it even more his fault, wouldn't it? "She fell over those rocks into the gorse. That's how she got all those scratches." He looked to Megan for support.

"Maybe. Yeah. Maybe she did." Megan didn't sound sure about anything. "I don't know," she admitted, blowing smoke. She was staring at the marks on her friend's face and neck.

"What are we going to do?" Glen wanted to know.

"One of us should go for help," Andy said.

"No, we should all go," Megan told him.

"We can't leave Lucy here."

Megan was shaking her head. "We'll have to carry her, but we should all go together."

"It'll be easier if just one of us goes, finds someone to help and brings them back," Andy said.

"But you don't know what attacked her," Megan said. "What if—"

"She *fell*, OK?" Andy snapped. "Nothing attacked her. Get real. What is there out here to attack her?"

"I can't believe we were all asleep," Megan said. "She might have been calling out to us or something."

The thought of this made Andy shiver, and for a few brief seconds he thought he might start to cry. He stared down at the limp, cold body of his girlfriend and felt sorry and useless and scared.

"I'll go for help," he said. "And when—"

"We should all go," Megan repeated.

"No, we shouldn't!" Andy shouted, suddenly angry. "I'll go. I'll go and find a farmhouse and get them to call for an ambulance. I'll go." And he was thinking, *Because it's my fault. I'll go because it's my fault.*

"I think we should all go," Glen said. He carried on quickly before Andy could bite his head off. "We don't know where we are, right? We're lost. So even if you do find a farmhouse or village or whatever, how are you going to find your way back here? Because you don't even know where *here* is."

Andy wanted to argue some more. He wanted to keep on shouting, but his shoulders sagged and he let out a heavy sigh. "Yeah, sorry. You're right," he said.

He tried to smile at his friend, but saw that Glen had tears in his eyes. One spilled over and ran down his cheek. Andy had to look away, biting his lip, fighting again to hold his own tears back. He realised Glen looked like he was ten years old again, like a little boy again.

"How did this happen?" Glen asked. "What did we do wrong?"

Andy sucked in a cold breath of damp air to steady himself. "Me and you will try to make some kind of stretcher out of the tents," he said. "Megan, can you just do your best to find out where we are on the map?"

"I'll be better with the map," Glen said.

Megan didn't say anything, so Andy just nodded and started to take down one of the tents.

The thick drizzle hung in the air like a mist, soaking them almost as badly as the rain had the day before.

Andy and Megan packed away their gear into the rucksacks, sharing Lucy's stuff between the three of them. They worked quickly. They laid one of the tents flat and folded it. Then, using the metal poles, they made a surprisingly good stretcher.

But all the time Andy kept going back to where Lucy lay in the sleeping bags. She looked as if she was asleep. He wanted to touch her, hold her. He thought of the gold heart he'd brought to give her, and what was written on the back of it. He'd always been too embarrassed to say those words out loud, but now he'd shout them at the top of his voice in the middle of a busy street, if it would make her wake up again.

Meanwhile, Glen had climbed back up to the top of the hill to try and get as good a view as possible, so he could work out where they were. When he came back the mist was hanging low over everything, covering the Moors. Andy didn't hold out much hope of Glen knowing which way to go. They had almost decided to follow the electricity pylons, because they must lead somewhere in the end. But then Glen found something on the map.

"We started out by going north from Hawnby, right?" he said.

Andy and Megan agreed.

"Well, look." He showed them the map, which was getting soggier by the second and seemed likely to fall apart if they weren't careful. "I don't think we've come nearly as far as we thought we had. I think we came this way, and at the top of that hill is a pile of stones," he pointed up the hill, "which is marked here, see? *Cairn.* And I think we're this side of it, looking that way."

"We must have walked further than that," Megan said.

Glen shook his head. "We were all mucking about, weren't we. Andy was running around chasing Lucy and nobody even looked at the map once. When it started raining, we were already lost. I reckon we've walked in a kind of C shape, because we followed the River Rye for a bit when we first set out, didn't we? But I think we're somewhere here now." He drew the way they had come on the map with his finger. "Because over there in that valley," he continued, "there's a stream." He pointed at the map. "And it could be this one here."

Andy squinted at it. Then he shrugged. "If you say so."

"Well, if it is, and if I'm right, then we're not too far away from this village here," Glen said, showing them. "At the edge of the rip."

Megan was peering at the map. "What's it called?"

All three of them tried to see.

Glen laughed suddenly, but not in a way that sounded as though the joke was at all funny. "You don't want to know," he said.

"Let me see." Andy wasn't in the mood for jokes.

"Do you know what I first thought when I saw those marks on Lucy's neck?" Glen asked. "I thought it looked like a vampire had got her."

"Glen ..." Andy sounded cross.

"And look, this village is called Fangdale Beck." He forced himself to laugh again. "*Fang*dale. Weird, isn't it?"

Andy didn't laugh. He found himself suddenly glancing down at those small but deep wounds on Lucy's neck. He felt a shiver run along his spine. He noticed Megan looking too.

He shook himself and tutted loudly. "Oh, for God's sake!" He shook his head and rolled his eyes. "This is serious. Lucy could be dying!" The words clogged up in his throat the second he tried to say them. He had to steady himself again. "Can we just get going?" he said quietly. "Can we just get Lucy to a doctor?"

He picked up one end of the makeshift stretcher and Glen silently grabbed the other. Megan picked up the heaviest rucksack. And at just after nine o'clock in the morning they headed in what they hoped was the right direction.

Chapter 4

Empty at Noon

They walked.

The thick cloud hung low over the Moors. The wind chilled them and there were spits of icy rain. They struggled with Lucy on the makeshift stretcher, stumbling over the rough ground and taking it in turns to carry her. They didn't say much, but saved their breath. Time was slipping by. They had to get Lucy to a doctor as quickly as possible.

But they were soon worn-out, and their arms ached. Most of all they were scared.

"Let me see the map," Andy said, suddenly.

The hills and moorland in front of them looked exactly the same as those they'd already walked through. They just didn't seem to be getting anywhere. "I want to see for definite where we're going."

He was sharing the stretcher with Megan and he nodded at her to lower her end. She did it gently, then rubbed at her sore hands as she moved away to rest on a grassy mound. She lit up yet another cigarette. She'd not said more than two words since they'd started walking.

Glen had the map. He'd already looked at it at least a dozen times in the past hour and it was getting ragged along the creases.

"We've been walking for nearly two hours and it all looks just the same," Andy complained, looking around him. "I can't work out where we are."

"We're going this way," Glen said, showing him on the map.

"Are you sure?" asked Andy. "How can you tell?"

All Glen could do was shrug.

Andy looked at Lucy's deathly pale face, with those horrible scratches. Her hair wasn't as blonde as he thought it should be. Or was it his imagination? The ends seemed to be turning grey. Was the colour fading? He told himself it was a trick of the light, nothing more.

Glen turned his back on Megan and lowered his voice to a whisper. "Do you think Megan's OK?"

Andy shrugged. "What do you mean?"

"Well, we don't really know her, do we?"

"She's Lucy's friend," Andy said.

Glen found it hard to put his thoughts into words. "How do we know she's telling the truth about last night? It's a bit strange that she didn't know Lucy was missing until this morning."

"She was asleep," Andy said. "Just like we were."

"How do you know?"

Andy would have laughed if it hadn't been for the serious look on his friend's face. "Are you saying Megan attacked Lucy?"

"Shh!" Glen hissed, worried Megan would hear. "We don't know who she is or anything. Lucy's never talked about her, has she?"

Andy shook his head in disbelief. "You're cracking up," he said. "First vampires, now this. Lucy fell, OK? Knocked herself out. Nothing or no-one attacked her."

Glen looked embarrassed and shuffled his feet. He was big and broad-shouldered, but Andy thought he was acting like a little kid.

"It's this place that's making you feel weird," Andy told him. He waved his arms around. "These Moors, with the mist and everything looking the same. Trust me, it's freaking me out just as bad." He glanced at Lucy's hair. "Let's just keep going, OK?"

Glen still didn't look happy, and when Megan came over to carry the stretcher again, he made sure he kept his distance.

"It's possible she was attacked," Megan said. "You don't get scratches on your neck like that from falling over."

"Depends how she fell," Andy insisted.

They walked on, taking turns with Lucy. Andy talked to her, hoping it would wake her up.

Another hour passed with the mist seeming to thicken around them. The sun was hidden by the heavy cloud but their watches said it was 12 o'clock. They didn't stop to eat what was left of their packed lunches, deciding to keep going while they could.

They had to struggle down a steep gully, all three of them carrying Lucy as their feet slipped and skidded on the wet grass. Their breath looked like ragged smoke in the cold air. The palms of their hands were red and raw from gripping the tent poles.

Megan was the first to see the farmhouse. It seemed to appear out of the mist bit by bit. First the dark slate of the roof, then the dull windows, then the solid wood door. There was a garage or stable to one side, a muddy driveway with a Land Rover sitting waiting like a well-trained dog.

Andy had never been more pleased to see anything in his life before. They all hurried towards it, almost running with the stretcher over the last few metres.

Andy and Glen laid the stretcher down. Megan banged on the heavy door. "Hello! Can you help us? Hello!"

"Knock harder," Andy told her.

Megan thumped with her fist. "HELLO! Is anybody there?"

Glen said, "Look at that. Above the door." There was a string of what looked like small onions across the top of the door. "Let's go. I don't want to stay here." He grabbed his end of the stretcher again.

"They might have a phone," Megan said.

Andy was staring at the string of bulbs. "Is that garlic?"

"Let's *go*," Glen insisted.

Andy looked from his friend to the garlic. Even he couldn't help thinking this was weird. Not that he was going to say so, because they couldn't walk away from the only house they'd come across all morning. This might be the only house for miles around.

"It's just superstition," he told Glen. "Vampires and garlic and all that. You know what people are like when they live in the middle of nowhere."

"Of course, yeah," Glen said, his voice shaking. "Superstition. Right. Here's Lucy with bite marks on her neck. And here's a farmhouse in a place called *Fangdale* with garlic above the door. Just superstition. Right."

Megan was staring at the garlic now. She'd stopped knocking and had stepped away from the door.

Andy threw up his hands in disgust. "What the hell is the matter with you two?"

"You've got to admit it's kind of weird," Megan said.

Andy didn't have to admit to anything. He peered in through the nearest window, cupping his hands against the glass. "I don't think there's anybody home." He pushed gently on the door and it swung open.

"Don't go inside," Glen said.

"I thought vampires didn't like garlic," Andy said, with a sarcastic smile. "Inside might be the safest place to be."

Glen blushed. He still didn't look happy, but he helped his friend carry the stretcher in through the open door.

"Hello?" Megan called. They were in a short hallway, a door on each side, with stairs rising up in front of them. "Anybody home? We need to use your telephone."

There was no answer.

Glen stayed with Lucy and the stretcher in the hallway, while Andy and Megan moved on tiptoe through the silent house.

In the living room somebody had left some knitting on the arm of the sofa. There was a mug of cold tea by the foot of a chair. There was a crucifix, like one they have in church, above the cold fireplace. In the kitchen the table was set for a meal. The fridge door hung open with the light on. Andy swung it closed. The dull thump it made seemed very loud in the silence.

Next to the kitchen was a small utility room with a washing machine. There was a pile of clean clothes in a basket on the floor, and an iron and ironing board had been set up.

They couldn't find a phone anywhere.

"They must have a phone," Andy whispered.

"Maybe not," Megan said.

"Let's go," Glen pleaded when they walked back into the hall.

Even Andy wanted to leave now. He didn't like this house. It felt all wrong somehow. But they had to make sure there wasn't a phone anywhere.

He crept upstairs, Megan close behind.

There was another crucifix on the landing wall. The bedroom was neat and tidy, the bed made. In the bathroom there was a full bath of cold water, as though somebody had run it and then simply walked away. A faded blue dressing gown hung on a hook on the back of the door.

They made their way back down to Glen and Lucy in the hallway. The only door that was locked was under the stairs. It was an odd shape, angled to fit the stairs' slope. Yet another crucifix had been nailed at the top.

Andy tried the handle but the door wouldn't budge.

"It probably leads to a basement or something," Megan said. "I doubt they'd have a phone down there."

Andy put his ear to the door. "Can you hear something moving?"

"Could be rats," Megan said, pulling a face. "Let's just go, can we?"

Andy surprised himself by not arguing. He was quite happy not to hang around. He'd felt like they were trespassing in someone else's house. And it felt as if whoever owned the house knew they were there. It felt as if they were being watched. He tried to ignore the feeling and told himself that it was just Glen's stupid stories that were getting to him.

They had a half-hearted look in the garage. No-one was at all shocked to find it empty except for bags of fertilizer and an old lawn mower.

The doors of the Land Rover were unlocked and they thought of taking it. But there were no keys and none of them knew how to hot-wire a car. Andy wished briefly that he'd hung around with the bad crowd at school.

Andy took the map this time. Megan and Glen carried Lucy.

The mist seemed to be clearing a little and they could see the farm track leading away over the Moors. Maybe if they stuck to the track it would come out onto a main road, or even lead them to a village.

Nobody complained that they hadn't found a phone at the farmhouse. Nobody said a thing as they turned their backs and kept walking. They wanted to put plenty of distance between them and the house.

Then maybe they could pretend that the weird feeling of being watched had been nothing more than their overactive imaginations.

Chapter 5
Four o'clock Rain

The Moors rolled on and on. The hills rose and fell. The three of them kept walking.

No cars passed as they trudged along the track. The mist had finally cleared, but only for the heavy rain to start. They huddled at the edge of a clump of trees for shelter. Andy held out his hands as if to catch the cold rain, but he was really hoping it would cool the painful blisters that had come up on his palms. Megan was kneeling in the mud next to Lucy. She'd run out of cigarettes and was chewing a big wodge of gum. She stroked

Lucy's hair. Andy didn't like to look at her hair now. He was sure the glorious blonde it had been only yesterday was fading away and the grey was spreading.

Glen hadn't said a word for almost two hours. He seemed to have hunched up into himself, like a tortoise retreating into its shell. He ate his last sandwich, watching Megan out of the corner of his eye. Andy was almost as worried about his best friend as he was about Lucy. If anything was truly weird around here, it was the way Glen was acting. The way he kept checking his watch seemed oddest of all.

"What time is it?" Andy asked.

Glen almost jumped out of his skin, surprised at suddenly being spoken to. "Nearly four," he managed to say.

"Is your watch battery running out?"

Glen was confused. "I don't think so."

"I just wondered why you keep checking it, that was all," Andy said.

Glen shrugged. "I want to know how long we've got left before it gets dark."

"We'll find somewhere before it gets dark," Andy assured him, hoping he sounded convincing. "This track has to lead somewhere, right?"

"I hope so," Glen said, sounding worried. "Because whatever attacked Lucy is still out there. And it could be following us."

Andy rolled his eyes. "You really are cracking up, aren't you?"

Glen was suddenly angry. "*You* explain it, then. Go on. Explain what happened to Lucy. Explain that farmhouse with the garlic and crucifixes and stuff. And the name. *Fang*dale."

Megan looked up. "Stop it," she said. "Let's just keep going. I hate this place and I'm scared enough as it is."

"Why should we listen to you?" Glen snarled at her. "We don't know you. Maybe *you've* got something to do with all this."

Megan laughed at him nastily. "Yeah, I'm a vampire all right. Can't you tell?" She bared her teeth. "Look at my fangs."

Andy had a hand on Glen's shoulder. He'd never seen his friend like this before. "Hey, come on, Glen. We're all feeling a bit freaked-out at the minute. But listen to what you're saying ..."

There was real fear in Glen's eyes when he asked, "What happens when it gets dark? What happens then?"

Andy didn't know what he meant.

Glen jabbed a finger at Lucy's pale, limp body wrapped up in the sleeping bags. "Let's just say she *has* been bitten by a vampire. Just pretend, OK? It means she's one too, doesn't it? And she'll wake up when it gets dark. And she'll come after us."

Andy wasn't sure if he believed what he was hearing. He looked over at Megan, and was shocked to see the colour drain from her face. "You're not serious?" he said. "Megan, tell him he's gone mad, will you?" But Megan didn't say a word. "Glen, come on ..."

Glen met his eyes and didn't look away.

Andy was trying to laugh, trying to make out it was the best joke he'd heard in ages. "So what do you want to do?" he asked. "Put a stake through her heart, just in case?"

Glen didn't answer yes or no, but dropped his eyes and stared at Lucy on the stretcher.

"Just shut up!" Andy shouted. "Shut up and grab the other end of the stretcher."

He waited for Glen to pick up the other end, but Glen didn't move.

"Come *on*! There's got to be another farmhouse on this track and we're not stopping until we find it."

Glen still didn't move towards the stretcher. He checked his watch again, and that was when Andy exploded. He charged at his friend and forced him to the ground. Glen was bigger than Andy, but Andy was on top. Glen kicked and thrashed. Andy grabbed his friend's wrist, twisting it up, making him yelp. He tugged at Glen's watch. He tore it off and threw it to the ground as Glen rolled over to one side, sending Andy sprawling. But Andy was on his feet quickly and he stamped down hard on the watch. He smashed it beneath his heel.

"Who cares *when* it gets dark!" he shouted. "Who cares?" He was panting, his chest heaving. "No-one cares, because nothing's going to happen, OK? No vampires! Nothing!"

Glen got to his feet slowly. He stood taller and broader than Andy. He clenched his fists.

Megan stepped in between them. "I thought you two were meant to be best friends," she said quickly. "I think we're all a bit stressed out at the minute. And being lost isn't helping. It's not helping us, and it's certainly not helping Lucy, is it? We should be getting her to a doctor. She's the important one."

Andy managed to get his breathing under control. "I have to help Lucy," he told Glen. "She's my girlfriend." And when he said that he could feel tears in his eyes. He thought about the gold heart again. "I love her," he said.

Glen blinked slowly.

"I'm sorry about your watch," Andy said. "I'll buy you a new one when we get home. Honest."

"*If* we get home," Glen said.

"We will. Of course we will," Andy told him. He attempted a smile. "And trust me, in the morning everything will be normal and you'll wake up and you'll suddenly remember what you said today. You'll want to crawl under a rock and die because you'll be so embarrassed about all of this."

Glen let his fists go limp. He scuffed the remains of his watch in the dirt with the toe of his trainer. "I think I'm cracking up," he said.

"You and me both." Andy grinned widely. But Glen wasn't smiling.

Andy took the rear of the stretcher, Glen picked up the front. Megan held Lucy's hand and walked by their side as they headed off into the rain again. The silence between the three of them was as heavy as the girl they carried.

Chapter 6

Creeping Twilight

At least two hours passed without anybody talking.

Andy's legs were so tired. His arms and shoulders ached terribly. The track twisted this way and that, seeming to bend back on itself and take them nowhere. All they could do was follow it as it rose and fell over the hills.

The rain had lightened to a drizzle once again and the sun was at last trying to make an appearance. But it was too late and it hung low in the sky. The map was so badly soaked that the paper was falling apart in several places. In other words, the map was useless.

Andy had no idea how far they'd walked, or in what direction they were going. Their only hope was the track and they clung to it.

The sun slipped lower. The sky was beginning to darken, and the fear of having to stay another night lost on the Moors was growing at the back of Andy's mind. He'd noticed the way Glen was watching the sky. Andy might have smashed his watch, but Glen was keeping a close eye on the sun getting lower and lower behind the hills.

Was his best friend cracking up? Andy shook his head, trying to rattle some sense into his own brain. It had been a rough day, no doubt about it. Maybe they were all going a bit mad. They were worn-out, scared, alone. Who wouldn't lose it, even a little bit?

"Put Lucy down," Megan said suddenly, waving her hands for them to lay the stretcher down. "She moved! She's waking up!"

Andy and Glen lowered the stretcher quickly but gently. Andy crouched over Lucy while Megan squeezed her hand. He could see Lucy's eyelids flickering.

Andy's heart beat faster. "Come on," he whispered. "Please. Please, wake up. Come on, Lucy. You can do it. Open your eyes."

In the fading daylight her hair looked almost completely grey now, not the blonde it used to be. Andy tried not to think about it, however, and stroked her cheek.

"She's waking up," Glen said.

"Yes," Megan replied, beaming widely. "Yes, she is."

Andy looked up at Glen, wanting to share a smile with him, but Glen was staring at the sun as it dropped below the hills. Their long shadows stretched across the track in front of them.

"She's waking up and it's getting dark," Glen said, in a matter-of-fact voice.

Andy was on his feet quickly. "Don't start that vampire stuff again," he said, hoping it came out light-hearted. "It's good news, OK. Nothing weird or scary. Lucy's coming round."

"Hey, Lucy. Open your eyes," Megan was saying gently.

Glen was walking away towards the nearest tree. Andy was following him, scared of what his friend might do. When Glen reached up to snap a branch from the tree, Andy was blocking his path back to Lucy.

"What the hell do you think you're doing?"

"Get out of my way," Glen said. He stripped the new leaves from the branch. He pulled off the small shoots until he had as close to a stake as he could make.

"You really have gone off your head, haven't you?" Andy said. "You've lost it. You're a nutter!"

"Look at her neck," Glen snarled. "What else could have done that to her neck?" He shoved Andy violently to one side and strode up to where Megan was crouched over Lucy. "Look at her hair," he said. "You're always going on about her blonde hair, but look at it now. It looks dead, but she's still breathing."

All Andy could say was, "You've gone mad. You're crazy." And to him it felt like the whole world had gone off the rails.

Megan looked up at Glen as he bent down over Lucy, the stake in his hand. "You can't do it, Glen. Think about it."

"If she wakes up we're all dead," Glen told her.

"You don't really believe in vampires, do you?"

Glen gripped the pointed branch and said nothing.

"Think about what you're doing, will you?" shouted Andy.

Megan stood up slowly, but kept herself between Glen and Lucy. "Listen to Andy," she begged Glen. "He's your best friend. He's right and you won't listen."

"I don't trust you either," Glen told Megan and pushed her out of the way.

Time seemed to slow down for Andy. Seconds seemed to take minutes to pass by. He tried to charge Glen as he stood over Lucy, but it felt as if it was taking hours to take those two or three simple steps. *This can't be happening*, his mind screamed. *This can't be happening!*

Glen stared down at Lucy as she made a soft groaning noise and her eyelids fluttered. He looked up to the sun, which had all but disappeared.

"Glen!" Megan wailed.

"No, Glen!" Andy shouted. "Don't you touch her!"

It was the sound of a car coming along the track that stopped anything from happening.

A beat-up Volvo estate rounded the bend out of the misty drizzle. The three of them stood still and silent and watched it approach along the rutted and bumpy track. An old lady with a flowery headscarf sat behind the wheel. She braked suddenly, the car juddered to a halt and she poked her head out of the driver's side window.

"Have you had an accident?" she asked. "Are you all right?"

Andy saw Glen let the makeshift stake drop to the ground, and took a shuddering breath of relief.

"We need help," he said to the old lady.

Chapter 7

Dark

The old lady was called Mrs Hooper. Lucy remained silent and limp as they lifted her into the car. Then Mrs Hooper drove them back to her house, a mile or so further along the track.

The three of them wrapped Lucy up and tucked her into the double bed in the spare room. Meanwhile, Mrs Hooper phoned for an ambulance. She warned them it might take a while for the ambulance to find its way out to her house. While they waited she sat them around her large wooden kitchen table and forced cups of sweet tea down them. She asked what had happened and listened politely to their story. Andy and Megan did most of the telling. Glen stayed quiet. Nobody felt the need to mention vampires. Andy had taken the gold heart out of his rucksack and was keeping it in his pocket. He wanted it to be the first thing Lucy saw when she woke up.

"My, it really does sound as if you've had quite an adventure," Mrs Hooper said. "I'm sure if it wasn't for the rain you would have been able to see just how close you must have come to some of the farms round here."

"There was one," Glen said, speaking for the first time. "But it was deserted. It was just as if whoever lived there had walked out in a hurry."

Andy tried to kick his friend under the table to shut him up. But he couldn't quite reach. He'd hoped that now they were back in civilisation, Glen would have calmed down a bit.

Mrs Hooper raised her eyebrows. "Walked out in a hurry?" she asked. "Oh no, I doubt it, my dear."

"The door was left open," Glen insisted.

"We don't have many burglars up here on the Moors," Mrs Hooper told him. "No-one bothers to lock up." She paused and added darkly, "Though if it's Fangdale Farm you're talking about, there's always gossip and rumours about that place."

She busied herself boiling the kettle again. "I'll make your friend a nice hot water bottle," she said. "She felt icy-cold. I'll put it in the bed with her. If any of you want to call your parents, the phone is on the table in the hall."

Andy and Megan thanked her.

When she had taken the hot water bottle upstairs, Andy rounded on Glen. "OK, it's all

71

over now. No more mucking about and doing your freaky vampire stuff. I'm phoning home and getting you back to reality as soon as possible."

Megan said, "I can't believe Lucy tried to set me up for a whole weekend with somebody who turned out to be such a weirdo."

Glen looked as though he'd been slapped in the face. He slowly put his head in his hands. "Everything feels so messed up," he said, slowly. "My head's spinning and I can't work out what's going on anymore."

"Tell me about it," Andy said.

He was about to say more, but there was a thump from upstairs. And then a terrified scream. Glass smashed.

The three of them were on their feet in an instant, charging through into the hall, taking the stairs two at a time.

"Lucy!" Andy was yelling.

The door to the spare room was closed. Andy hit it with his shoulder but it hardly moved. Something was blocking it from the other side. Glen pushed him out of the way and managed to force it open after two or three attempts.

What they saw froze them to the spot.

The bed was empty. The window had been smashed. Lucy was gone.

Mrs Hooper was sprawled on the floor with the hot water bottle spilling steaming water across the carpet.

Andy and Megan ran to the broken window. The chill wind blew in around them. It was completely dark outside now, the only light came from the house. The dirt track and the fields and the Moors beyond were in pitch blackness. But Andy thought he saw a figure running deeper into the night.

"Lucy?" he murmured.

Glen was kneeling down next to Mrs Hooper. "Look at this," he said. "Andy, come and look at this!"

Andy turned to see Glen cradling the old lady's head. There were two scarlet wounds on her neck. They were almost identical to the ones they'd seen on Lucy.

Megan let out a small whimper. Andy felt faint; he thought he was going to crack up completely. He looked back out of the window, to the darkness of the Moors.

"Lucy," he whispered. "Lucy."

Megan was crouched in the corner shaking and sobbing. There was the crack and snap of wood being broken. Andy turned towards Glen who was holding a jagged and splintered chair leg over Mrs Hooper.

Glen nodded down at the old lady. "Are you going to do it, or am I?" he asked.

74

Barrington Stoke would like to thank all its readers for commenting on the manuscript before publication and in particular:

Daniel Alves	Christine Johnson
Joe Belton	Andrew Leadbitter
Matthew Belton	Kayleigh MacDonald
Aaron Bolton	Craig Maison
Hannah Cameron	Steph Moore
Katrina Challenger	Priona Naidoo
Anthony Cheng	Mary Nicholson
Catherine Coats	Daniel Oram
Sabrina Corcoran	Danielle O'Reilly
Stacey D'Souza	Catherine Stirling Hill
Michael Gordon	Clare Wade
Mrs M. Harrison	Kyra White
Gary Henshall	

Become a Consultant!

Would you like to give us feedback on our titles before they are published? Contact us at the address or website below – we'd love to hear from you!

Barrington Stoke, 10 Belford Terrace, Edinburgh EH4 3DQ
Tel: 0131 315 4933 Fax: 0131 315 4934
E-mail: info@barringtonstoke.co.uk
Website: www.barringtonstoke.co.uk

More Teen Titles!

Joe's Story by Rachel Anderson 1-902260-70-8
Playing Against the Odds by Bernard Ashley 1-902260-69-4
Harpies by David Belbin 1-842990-31-4
Firebug by Eric Brown 1-842991-03-5
TWOCKING by Eric Brown 1-842990-42-X
To Be A Millionaire by Yvonne Coppard 1-902260-58-9
All We Know of Heaven by Peter Crowther 1-842990-32-2
Walking with Rainbows by Isla Dewar 1-842991-30-2
The Ring of Truth by Alan Durant 1-842990-33-0
Falling Awake by Viv French 1-902260-54-6
The Wedding Present by Adèle Geras 1-902260-77-5
The Cold Heart of Summer by Alan Gibbons 1-842990-80-2
The Shadow on the Stairs by Ann Halam 1-902260-57-0
Alien Deeps by Douglas Hill 1-902260-55-4
Partners in Crime by Nigel Hinton 1-842991-02-7
The New Girl by Mary Hooper 1-842991-01-9
Dade County's Big Summer by Lesley Howarth 1-842990-43-8
Runaway Teacher by Pete Johnson 1-902260-59-7
No Stone Unturned by Brian Keaney 1-842990-34-9
The House of Lazarus by James Lovegrove 1-842991-25-6
Wings by James Lovegrove 1-842990-11-X
A Kind of Magic by Catherine MacPhail 1-842990-10-1
Stalker by Anthony Masters 1-842990-81-0
Clone Zone by Jonathan Meres 1-842990-09-8
The Dogs by Mark Morris 1-902260-76-7
Turnaround by Alison Prince 1-842990-44-6
Dream On by Bali Rai 1-842990-45-4
What's Your Problem? by Bali Rai 1-842991-26-4
All Change by Rosie Rushton 1-902260-75-9
Fall Out by Rosie Rushton 1-842990-74-8
The Blessed and The Damned by Sara Sheridan 1-842990-08-X
Double Vision by Norman Silver 1-842991-00-0